D0296792

EELIE AND
THE BIG CATS

by the same author

TIGER HAVEN

TARA: A TIGRESS

PRINCE OF CATS

TIGER! TIGER!

EELIE AND THE BIG CATS

Billy Arjan Singh

Drawings by Pat Marriott

JONATHAN CAPE
THIRTY-TWO BEDFORD SQUARE LONDON

First published 1987

Jonathan Cape Ltd, 32 Bedford Square, London WC1B 3EL

British Library Cataloguing in Publication Data

Singh, Billy Arjan
Eelie and the big cats.
1. Leopards —— Biography 2. Tigers
—— Biography 3. Mammals —— India
—— Uttar Pradesh —— Biography
I. Title
599.74'428 QL795.L5

ISBN 0-224-02489-2

Printed in Great Britain by
Butler & Tanner Ltd,
Frome and London

Contents

PAKISTAN
Dudhwa
Delhi
Lucknow
Calcutta
INDIA
Bombay
Madras

Billy Arjan Singh is one of India's leading big-cat specialists, who has devoted the past thirty years to the welfare of leopards and tigers in the forests behind his home at Dudhwa, on the border of Nepal.

In this short book, cast in the form of a letter, he recalls his association with Eelie, the little mongrel who came to him as a stray and stayed for the rest of her life.

To Billy she was 'the ultimate dog', for she did what none of her species had ever done before – formed close relationships with the leopards and the tiger which he reared in and around the house, and lived with the great cats on equal terms before they took to the wild.

This eloquent and moving memoir recalls a unique association.

ONE

A Stranger Arrives

Tiger Haven,
Northern India.

My dear Eelie,

First, let me explain why I am writing you this letter. My aim is to spend some hours in your company, and, in thinking about you, to recall the exciting times that we shared together. Also, of course, I want other people who never knew you to see what an exceptional creature you were.

As you knew better than anyone, dogs get a raw deal in India: millions are born every year, ownerless and unwanted, a mixture of breeds innumerable, and almost all become pariahs, or social outcasts. Mangy and rickety, nourished on rubbish and dehydrated hides, they are known as pye-dogs and chased away from human homes, to stagger through a portion of their expected life-span as rejects; then, all too often, they are run over on public highways, and their poor broken bodies are picked at by scavenging crows and vultures.

That would almost certainly have been your lot, had fate not thrown us together. Where you came from I shall never know, but I remember the morning of your arrival as if it were yesterday. A fiery sun had just risen from behind the low line of trees that form the eastern horizon at Tiger Haven, my home on the edge of the jungle. To the north, behind the screen of sal trees which towered straight and tall above the Escarpment, thunder-heads muttered and growled among the mountains of Nepal, for the monsoon had been late that summer, and although it was already October, we were still getting occasional storms.

As usual in the early morning, I was sitting out on the river-bank with a cup of tea. Below me mist seethed and billowed over the surface of the Junction Pool as the sun struck the chill waters of the Neora and Soheli rivers at the point where they flow together. Flights of green parrots went whistling overhead as they left their roost in the forest and headed for their feeding-grounds.

Then I noticed a posse of men approaching – a gang of labourers on their way to repair earth roads that had been washed away by the monsoon floods. They were led by a Forest Guard clad in khaki, and behind them, bringing up the rear, came a forlorn and diminutive sandy-coloured creature which looked like a jackal. Only the jaunty twist of its tail, which stood up straight and curled over at the top, and the fact that the animal accompanied humans, showed it was a dog.

Thus it was that I first set eyes on you, a poor plebeian outcast. The Forest Guard, an old friend, paused briefly for a chat before going on his way. I watched him and his men plod off into the trees, but as I gazed I felt that something was missing from the picture, and I realised the dog was no longer with them.

A movement caught my eye. I looked round, and there you sat. I could not be sure how old you were – perhaps six months; but you were so miserably thin that every rib was visible under your skin, and your hip bones stuck out like a pair of clothes-pegs. When you stood up and walked, a slight limp showed that even the saucy set of your tail had probably been caused by malnutrition or by a blow or kick from some unfeeling passer-by. But out of a pert and perky face there shone a pair of lustrous, black-rimmed eyes, and as you ingratiatingly accepted a piece of toast, I knew you had come to stay. At once the peculiar shape of your tail suggested a name: because it reminded me of an eel, I called you Eelie.

My mother, from whom I had inherited my love of animals, was living with me in those days; and because I had recently lost a Labrador who had been with me for twelve years, she felt sure that I would not want to keep another dog. She therefore asked one of her servants to drive the newcomer away. You, however, dodged all the missiles and stayed on, to become everybody's favourite.

In fact the person who saved you was my nephew Jairaj, known as Tiggy, who was staying with us at the time. It was he who defied my mother and stood up for you; in spite of her orders to the household staff, he went and got you a meal and began to look after you.

With proper feeding, your condition very soon improved, but then you became ill with a virulent form of mange, which reduced whole areas of your body to raw, bleeding skin. Of course I was extremely worried, and wondered if your sudden change of diet had brought on the dermatitis. Luckily Tiggy cared for you with the greatest dedication, and daily baths of sulphur soap helped you to recover and grow a beautiful new coat, though it took you about three months to do so.

Restored to health, you quickly proved yourself hardy, intelligent and affectionate without being demonstrative – in fact everything that I could have wanted in the way of an animal companion – for you at once became my closest confederate. Being a bachelor, and living on my own except for the small farm staff and a few household servants, I welcomed the arrival of a partner who could share my solitary existence and who joined in my jungle patrols with such obvious enjoyment.

Soon I could see that you had quite a talent for languages: almost always I would talk to you in English, but you also understood many words in Hindustani – and none better than *khana*, or food, which you would pick up in the middle of a human conversation, even if it was not addressed to you.

Over the years you mothered many a family, and once distinguished yourself by rearing a litter of seven. You became so well-known locally that in a country where no one normally has any use for female puppies, your offspring were all assured of homes. Of course I now wish that I had kept at least one of your children – but I always felt that no other dog could replace you, no matter how like you it might be.

In the thirteen years we were together you built a unique bridge between the domestic world of man and the wild world of tigers, leopards, wolves, fishing cats and monkeys. You attained a unique moral ascendancy over the dread predators of the forest, who were many times your size, and you never hesitated to drive them off their legitimate kills in a way that has surely never been equalled. You proved that, if left in peace, animals both wild and domestic can live together in harmony – and that, to my mind, is a lot for a canine waif to prove.

It occurs to me that readers who do not know us may well wonder what I *do* – what my profession is. All I can say is that I am a freelance wildlife enthusiast, and that I have devoted the past thirty years of my life to the welfare of the great cats, principally leopards and tigers.

In my youth I shot game with enthusiasm – something of which I am now neither proud nor ashamed, for it was simply a fact of life. I was brought up in the state of Balrampur, where my father had been appointed by the Government to look after the affairs of the Maharajah, who was then a minor, and shooting was something to which every growing boy was introduced as a matter of course. Thus I killed my first leopard at the age of twelve, and my first tiger at fourteen.

But as I grew older, the desire to kill was replaced by a desire to keep – to preserve the wild animals which were dwindling at an alarming rate as the great forests in which they lived were eroded by an ever-increasing human population. When the Second World War ended in 1945 I became a farmer, but in 1959 I decided I wanted to live closer to the forest, and so moved to Tiger Haven, where I am now. On a lovely, park-like site at the very edge of the jungle, as far from civilisation as it was possible to go, I put up a line of low, white buildings which I gradually extended and improved to make a simple yet comfortable home.

No one would call Tiger Haven smart, but almost everyone who comes here seems to like the place. Readers may think it sounds rather primitive if I say that the electricity supply is extremely irregular, and often breaks down, and that our hot water is heated in a 45-gallon oil drum over a wood fire outside the back of the house; but visitors agree that there are few things more luxurious than to have a steaming hot bath in a big tin tub, by candlelight, with a couple of buckets of scalding water standing beside you, from which to top up the brew.

In front of the house there is a strip of grass, kept short by grazing animals, and then fields of rice and barley, on which peacocks and junglefowl (the ancestors of farmyard chickens) feed in the early mornings. Beyond the fields, perhaps three hundred yards away, is a wall of high, wild grass, some ten feet tall, which is the favourite resort of the small hog-deer. Immediately behind the house is the River Neora, and just beyond its narrow stream, on the far bank, the jungle.

It was here, at my sanctuary on the edge of the forest, that you arrived on that beautiful autumn morning, and here that, to my incalculable benefit, you decided to remain.

TWO

Monkey Business

You settled into the routine of Tiger Haven within a few days. It must have been an enormous change for you, as you had been born – I presume – in some village near the farmland. Now you were living right on the edge of the jungle: as we set off on our daily walks the first few steps took us out of the domain of man and into that of the forest animals.

For a small and inexperienced dog, it was a world full of dangers: leopards, for instance, rate dogs high on their list of delicacies, and a chance encounter with one could easily have been fatal for you. Unless there is some emergency – such as when a man-eating tiger has made a kill – I never carry a gun in the forest; and even if I had been armed on our walks, it would probably not have saved you, for the attack-charge of a leopard or tiger normally consists of no more than a couple of lightning bounds, and the odds are that I would not have been able to react quickly enough to divert an assault.

But, no matter what your immediate background had been, the age-old instincts which you carried in your genes served you well, and you assessed your new environment with remarkable speed. I remember particularly the intense concentration with which you studied the scent-patterns left by animals during their night's activities – the places where a tiger had scraped the ground or sprayed urine on a tree-trunk, marking his territory; the remains of some predator's kill; the excavations of wild pigs; or the small piles of droppings left by deer. Without even a mother to instruct you, you knew at once that it was safe to chase the chital, or spotted deer, but that any manifestation of tiger or leopard demanded maximum wariness.

In fact, you came into contact with forest animals without even leaving the immediate environs of Tiger Haven, for in those days I kept two elephants – one called Bhagwan Piari – which means 'The Beloved of God' – and the other Sitara, or 'Star'. At nine foot tall and maybe five tons in weight, they must have seemed veritable monsters to someone of your modest dimensions. Yet far from being intimated by them, you treated them as coolly as if you had lived with elephants for years.

Apart from this, your first close encounter with forest creatures came not at Tiger Haven, but at Jasbirnagar Farm, where I had lived when I first settled in the area, some eight miles to the south. Because the land round Tiger Haven is low-lying, it always floods during the monsoon in June, July and August, as water pours down out of the mountains in the north and the local rivers burst their banks. Often the house is completely surrounded by water; and in those days I used to move to Jasbirnagar, together with the elephants, for a few weeks to escape the worst of the rains.

That year – your first monsoon – I shifted my quarters in the middle of June, just before communication with the outside world was severed. Already established at Jasbirnagar were two rhesus monkeys, one known as Sister Guptara, because she reminded us of a nurse in a hospital, and the other as Elizabeth Taylor, so called because she had a pretty face and natural traces of blue, which looked like make-up, above her eyes. I was worried that you might grab them, particularly Sister Guptara, whose left arm had been withered by a severe electric shock when she climbed a transformer pole, so that she was a little less agile than her companion. Sure enough, the moment you saw them, you put in a charge and chased them up the teak trees planted round the house. But as you got to know them, and they you, an easy camaraderie established itself.

Everyone seemed to feel particularly sociable first thing in the morning, when the family gathered on the verandah for tea. You would sit on the ground, the monkeys would perch on the edge of an upturned bed or on the backs of chairs, and all of you would get a little hand-out in the form of a piece of toast or a biscuit. Although the atmosphere was usually amicable, sometimes one of the monkeys would decide that her sister was getting favoured treatment and push her off her seat – whereupon a petulant argument would break out, with much spitting and screeching.

Soon the removal of the tea-tray became the signal for communal games. You would chase Guptara from chair to bed and back, and she would sit just out of reach, grimacing and jerking her scalp back and forth as only primates seem capable of doing. Elizabeth Taylor meanwhile would seize the end of your tail and with an expression of furious concentration on her face rush round and round like some crazed hammer-thrower as you, in mock-frustration, chased both tail and Taylor. One morning, just before tea, all three of you appeared in the most ridiculous procession. Guptara was riding on your back, and behind you came Elizabeth Taylor, walking up the stairs on her hind legs and holding on to your tail with her hands, as if carrying the train of some important personage.

These games, with slight variations, developed into a regular feature of the morning. Afterwards it was time for grooming, in which the monkeys pulled imaginary delicacies from each other's coats. This session would also usually end in a noisy altercation, when someone thought her hair had been pulled with unnecessary violence.

Eventually, as the stifling, moist heat of the monsoon wore on, the whole pattern changed when Sister Guptara went off with a husband and Elizabeth Taylor appeared one day with a small son in tow. Now a young mother, she was naturally protective of her offspring, and, lacking the moral support of her former companion, would sit on the branch of a low tree and tease you or try to pull your ears.

By the time you and I returned to Tiger Haven at the end of the rains, the baby had grown into a good-sized and precocious little macaque. Mother and son spent most of their day away from the house, but in the evenings they would come back, for they knew that the elephants would have had their *rotis*, or cakes of unleavened bread, and that a few bits could probably be scrounged. Once we had left, and the house stood empty, the monkeys abandoned it, no longer finding food and affection there; for weeks I was haunted by the picture of them returning in the dusk, perched on the back of draught buffaloes like children coming home for supper, and I wished I had brought them to Tiger Haven with us.

Perhaps I could have. Already, by adapting so quickly to life with the monkeys, you had reinforced my belief that it is possible for animals of one species to form lasting relationships with those of another, even though most people would expect the two to be mutually hostile. Even so, it was with some trepidation that I embarked on what turned out to be one of the great experiments of my life.

THREE

Prince of Cats

To introduce you to two small monkeys was one thing, but to bring a leopard into the household seemed an altogether more desperate venture, for this was a carnivore with an awesome reputation. I myself was educated in Naini Tal, a town in the foothills of the Himalayas, and there I was lucky enough to see a good deal of the legendary hunter-naturalist Jim Corbett, whose book *Man-Eaters of Kumaon* has become a classic of jungle literature. Sitting at his feet as a boy, I heard many stories of how dogs were the favourite food of leopards, and how these furtive hill predators abducted pets from the very feet of their masters or mistresses.

It is perfectly true that leopards will snatch dogs or goats from among the huts of a village; but I did not know then that such attacks are generally caused by a lack of wild prey-species such as deer, pigs and monkeys in the forest round about. Nor did I know that leopards are tremendous survivors, and will do their utmost to adapt to whatever situation they find themselves in. (Even so, the leopards round Naini Tal lost out in the end, and there are none left in that area, once so magical, which has now become a crowded and polluted holiday-resort.)

Nevertheless, in spite of the obvious risks, I had no hesitation in accepting the offer of a young leopard, which had been found abandoned as a cub in Bihar and was reared in Calcutta by Anne Wright and her daughter Belinda (Blue) – two outstanding conservationists. My aim in taking the animal on was to see if I could bring him up and set him free in the wild, and so make a small but perhaps valuable contribution to the dwindling leopard population in the forest behind my home.

By the time he was four months old, the cub had grown too big and obstreperous to live any longer in the Wrights' compound in the city, so they brought him by train to Lucknow, where I met them in my jeep. Already he was quite large – about three feet six inches long, including his tail – and strongly spotted (the Hindustani for leopard, *guldar*, means literally a rose – in other words, an animal covered with rosettes).

Imagine my anxiety during the long drive back to Jasbirnagar! As we approached the house, the first thing I saw was you and the two monkeys, alerted by the sound of our engine and formed up on the steps of the verandah as a kind of reception committee.

The next few minutes were very tense. We got out of the vehicle, Anne Wright holding the leopard on a collar and leash. You came up and gave me a perfunctory greeting, but then immediately tried to nip the cub in the rump. The monkeys took up threatening postures and then retreated on to an awning, where they continued their grimaces, working their scalps up and down with expressive rapidity. The leopard, surrounded on three sides by hostile demonstrations, grinned nervously.

You continued to be very aggressive all that day, and Anne became despondent. 'It isn't going to work,' she said. 'Eelie will never accept him.'

But she was wrong. On the second day the atmosphere was calmer. On the third you and the cub went off together to explore some nearby bushes, and acceptance seemed to be complete. I felt immensely relieved, and also grateful to you for having achieved a minor miracle.

When the leopard arrived, he was called Cheetla, but almost at once I re-named him Prince, for to me the leopard was – and is – the prince of cats. His relationship with you went from strength to strength, but with the monkeys he never settled down so well, chiefly because of their fidgety and erratic movements, which inevitably triggered his instinct to attack. (In all big cats the impulse to attack is often set off by sudden movement – which is why, if one comes face-to-face with a tiger in the jungle, it is far better to stand still or move very slowly than it is to run.)

One day, just as I was hoping that armed neutrality might give way to a more stable relationship, Prince grabbed hold of Sister Guptara and held on to her. I got her free, but after that his intentions towards the monkeys were definitely hostile: he was constantly chasing them up trees, and it became obvious that amicable co-existence was not going to be possible. I therefore decided that I must shift him to Tiger Haven and leave the monkeys behind.

Our journey was quick and uneventful, but it led to a fascinating sequel. You – as I am sure you remember – sat in front of the jeep with me, while Prince rode behind, in the space left empty by the removal of the back seat. The route from Jasbirnagar to Tiger Haven takes (if you will forgive the expression) the shape of a dog-leg, and the distance is about ten miles. First we drove east for three miles, and then turned left, towards the north, for another seven. We all arrived in good shape, and we spent that night together on the verandah, you and Prince sleeping on either side of my bed.

Next morning, however, I got a nasty shock, for you had vanished. A local search revealed no sign of you, and as it seemed impossible that the small leopard could have consumed you entirely at one sitting, without leaving any trace of the meal, I could only conclude that you had made your own way back to Jasbirnagar. The idea worried me greatly, for until then you had only done the journey in a vehicle; moreover, you were hampered by the limp in your left hind leg, and along the way you would be at risk from wild animals and fierce, semi-domesticated dogs.

I drove back to Jasbirnagar, and there to my great relief, I found you safely ensconced near the front porch with your two old friends, Elizabeth Taylor and Sister Guptara. It looked as if you had been telling them how much you preferred their company to that of the leopard, and the open spaces of the farmland to the close, dense world of the forest. Still, you also seemed pleased to see me, and hopped eagerly into the jeep for the return journey.

From your tracks, which we later found leading away from Tiger Haven, it was obvious that you had set off on your cross-country journey along the hypotenuse of the right-angle prescribed by the roads that we had driven together. In other words, a direction-finding ability unknown to us humans had guided you to your destination, across land you had never explored before. I was very much impressed, especially when I thought of how heavily humans rely on maps and compass-bearings and the constellations of the night sky for guidance on even short and simple journeys.

Since that day I have thought a great deal about the direction-finding powers of wild creatures which function so perfectly and never seem to break down – the fantastic migratory sense of birds, which fly for thousands of miles over continents and oceans, and the unerring ability of leopards and tigers to find their kills, on the darkest of nights and in the thickest of cover, even when they have travelled for hours since leaving them. More and more I realise how much of our original instinct we human beings have lost with the development of speech and thought; and the disparity was brought home to me as never before when I read a book called *The Soul of an Ape* by the South African author André Marais.

In this he describes how, as an experiment, six trained trackers and one packhorse trekked from A to B – a distance of two hundred miles across the open veld. Along the way they marked their route and the campsites at which they stayed overnight. In due course they reached their destination; but then heavy rain washed out all the landmarks they had left, and on the return journey the six men – for all their training – were completely at sea. The only member of the team still quite confident was the horse, who not only returned straight back the way he had come, but halted at the site of every camp – showing that he retained instincts long since lost by his more sophisticated companions. A different set of experiments showed that people who are hypnotised can regain a sense of direction, which otherwise remains submerged.

Fortunately, that single, unscheduled return to Jasbirnagar seemed to reassure you, and you settled down at Tiger Haven in Prince's company. There was nearly a year's difference in your ages – the leopard was four months old when he arrived, and you about fifteen – but you were still both growing up, and I am sure the fact that you were immature made it easier for you to forge links of friendship across the gap between your two species. All that I, the human, had to do was to exercise a measure of control.

In my company the association between you and Prince grew naturally. At night you slept on one side of my bed, on a straw palliasse, and Prince on the other. One particularly dark night, never to be forgotten, I woke up with the feeling that something was amiss. My torch-beam revealed both dog and leopard sitting bolt upright in bed with attention focussed on the floor. Looking down, I saw a large, black and yellow banded krait – one of the most venomous snakes in India – slithering past

my bed. Neither of you moved as I jumped up and killed the snake with a stick: instinct evidently told you to give it a wide berth.

Later, as Prince grew in confidence, he began to yearn for his night-time freedom – for his kind are mainly nocturnal animals – and took to tearing up his bedding in frustration. I therefore released him, and soon he was spending the nights up trees or on the roof of the building. You, on the other hand, remained content to sleep beside me – and indeed you became steadily more possessive about our sleeping area, resisting any attempt by the big cat to tear my bedding or even to approach the *sanctum sanctorum*. Both of you, I realised, were showing territorial instincts, but the manifestations were entirely different.

As the familiarity between the pair of you grew, you would set off into the forest together to hunt, and although each pursued his or her own method, you made a surprisingly successful team. During the chital fawning season in early winter you yourself would chase a nursing mother while Prince waited to pounce on any animal that became confused by your initial attack: on at least three occasions he grabbed a fawn which had panicked and got entangled in creepers.

I should explain that there is one major difference between the Indian jungle, which is sub-tropical, and the forests of countries with cooler climates. In our forests, although many of the trees are broad-leaved, including the majestic sal (a hardwood rather like mahogany), and the jamun, which grows best on the moist ground along river-banks, the leaves do not all fall at the same time, as in an English or American autumn. Instead, they are being renewed continuously, with the result that the jungle is never left bare and transparent, even in the winter, but remains thick and difficult to see through.

I was fascinated to find that even at a most tender age Prince had acquired the wisdom which makes all leopards take their prey up into trees, to preserve it from scavenging competitors such as tigers, hyaenas and vultures. There is no doubt that animals adopt subterfuges which enable them to exist with the minimum of effort; and I have heard that in Sri Lanka, where the leopards are the only major predators, they have no need to take their prey into trees, and so do not bother. But at Tiger Haven this habit became the source of great frustration to you, Eelie, for often you would finish your diversionary chase only to find leopard and prey already in a tree, and I would discover you gazing disconsolately upwards as Prince enjoyed his meal. By no means every operation was successful, however: I remember one occasion on which you caught a young chital stag and between you pinned it to the ground, but then displayed your immaturity by coming in search of me – whereupon the stag got up and departed.

Having never brought up a leopard before, I took advice from anyone able to give it; so when I was told by a zoo authority that roughage in the form of bird feathers was an essential item in a leopard's diet, I began going out into the jungle with a .22 rifle to shoot a parrot or a dove. Soon I found that you and Prince had similar tastes: neither of you would touch a mynah or a coucal (a kind of dowdy pheasant with a strong, bitter scent), but doves and parrots were universally popular – so much so that a strong element of competition quickly entered our joint operations.

I was intrigued to see how quickly you both learnt to associate the crack of a shot with the fall of a bird. Whenever I put the rifle up, both of you would watch me with intense expectation, and the shot might have been the crack of a starting-pistol, such was the speed of take-off. Usually you were quickest off the mark; but I am sorry to have to confess that I tried to make you come off second-best. As the whole exercise was being conducted for the benefit of the leopard, I would try to manoeuvre Prince into the best possible position before I fired – and if he reached the kill first, he would take it up a tree to eat it. What happened if *you* won the race, I was never quite sure, for you would disappear into the undergrowth and I never saw how you dealt with a bird. It was remarkable that, in spite of the strongly competitive atmosphere, there was never any unpleasantness, and the rule of finders-keepers was almost always observed – though I must admit that the leopard was normally the more forbearing of the two of you.

It was a strange feeling to go hunting with two such different animals, and I am willing to bet that Prince was the only gun-trained leopard in the world, then or since. It was not for several weeks that I realised the futility of the entire proceeding: then one day I found him carefully plucking a dove, pulling out feathers with his teeth and so rejecting the allegedly-indispensable roughage. Even so, both of you regarded our shooting forays as serious business, and one morning, when I missed shot after shot, I could feel the increasing tension with which you were both waiting for something to fall. In the end Prince could bear it no longer, and as I took aim at a dove for the tenth time he leapt on my back and knocked me flying. I could almost hear him say, 'What on earth do you think you're playing at?'

When Prince was ten months old, I decided to move him away from Tiger Haven to a base deeper in the forest, where he would be less disturbed by humans and more part of the jungle. I therefore built him a substantial tree-platform, or machan, about a mile to the west of the farm, and called the place Leopard Haven. This meant that the pattern of all our lives changed. Once Prince was

Tara and Eelie playing in the river

Eelie guarding Tiffany, the fishing kitten

Eelie getting the better of Harriet

established on the machan, he based himself there, and you and I would walk out together to visit him every morning and evening. Sometimes, also, he would pay us return visits and appear at the farm.

It was not long before a tigress realised that a new competitor had arrived to share her range, and she took to visiting Leopard Haven, sometimes spraying her scent-mark on one of the trees that supported the platform. In spite of his urban upbringing, Prince knew very well that the master-predator represented a potentially-lethal danger; and whenever the tigress had paid a visit we would find him at the very top of one of the trees, waiting for the reassurance that we brought before venturing down.

You, on the other hand, never seemed the least scared of these pungent visiting-cards – probably because you knew by instinct that a tigress was not a natural enemy. In fact, in my view, you soon became extremely reckless, disappearing off into the forest on your own for up to half an hour at a time, and ignoring my calls, which grew more and more agitated. Either you were extremely fortunate, or your own confidence was well justified, for you always returned unharmed in the end.

The contrast between your reactions and Prince's was again very marked when we all visited one of the tigress's kills together – the remains of a sambhar deer lying in some bushes and stinking to high heaven. For the first time the young leopard sprayed the trunk of a tree – a means of releasing tension – and then raced up it with a series of grunts that were clearly inspired by fear, whereas you calmly stayed behind to scavenge a bit of meat off the carcase.

By then the overpowering heat of the Indian summer was setting in. All the same, I kept up our daily walks, as I thought it vital to continue Prince's education. My main problem, when he arrived, had been to induce him to enter the forest at all. He seemed scared of the close, green world of the jungle – and yet it was essential, if he was to live free, for him to feel completely at home in it. I therefore did what I could to carry on his training.

Usually, as you and I walked out in the morning, we would find the leopard waiting for us on his platform. When he saw us approaching, he would come down and, after suitable greetings – touching noses with you, rubbing himself against my legs – he would fall in with us. Then, as it grew really hot, I found that you would still follow me, although you obviously found walking in such a temperature most unpleasant, but Prince, with the true independence of a cat, would climb a tree and refuse to come any further.

One morning in May I set out to photograph a tigress which had recently escaped from a gin-trap set by poachers. (She had been photographed in the trap – and the picture was so striking that it was later used on a World Wildlife Fund poster – luckily she had managed to wrench her paw free.) Now she was living to the west of Tiger Haven, and I hoped to find her cooling off in a certain stretch of the river.

As I made my way there, the day was so hot, and I was so intent on my errand, that I passed Leopard Haven without a backward glance. When I reached my destination – a bend where the river had carved the Escarpment into a sheer, sandy face which I named the White Cliffs – the tigress was indeed in the water, but she must have heard some slight sound that I made in approaching, for she moved off into cover. Then *I* heard a sound behind me, and, turning, saw that Prince had followed me after all.

For a moment I was disappointed: my chance of photographing the tigress had gone for the moment. But what followed was pure magic, for suddenly, to my amazement, Prince took to the river himself. Everything I had heard and read until then told me that leopards hated water – but here was a member of the species enjoying himself hugely, and for an hour he cavorted in the river with the greatest enthusiasm.

Next morning, instead of trying to stick to our usual routine, I took you and Prince straight to the river – and as I look back I think that the scenes which ensued were among the most rewarding of my life, for it was sheer delight to watch you both playing in the water.

Under the lee of the White Cliffs you would chase each other furiously on the gleaming sand and then rush into the river, where, with huge bounds, you would both plunge about after the pieces of wood that came eddying down the current. Sheets of spray flew into the air, lighting up in the sun with all the colours of the rainbow.

Then, after cooling off immersed to his ears in the stream, Prince would try to entice others to join him in his watery antics. His eyes would gleam with mischief as he leapt at me and my camera, and you would instinctively try to head him off by barking and nipping. Another favourite trick of his was to climb a slender tree which grew on the bank, and which would bend further and further over until it dumped him in the water. He never tired of this simple game – and he would alternate it with frantic chases, in which you and he pursued each other wildly up and down the beach. Even to me, who by then was used to seeing a leopard and a dog playing together, it was a fantastic sight, for Prince already weighed over seventy pounds and was about five feet six inches long. Had he wanted, he could have killed or disabled you in a second, yet there was never any question of that, such was the trust and affection between you. Watching you together, I began to realise that each of you saw the other not as a leopard or a dog, but as an individual being. It was almost as if, in the forging of this unique bond, species had ceased to matter.

That first day by the river, when the time came for you and me to go home, Prince did not come with us, but climbed a tree, having evidently decided that the place suited him. When we returned in the evening he was still there, and over the next few days it became clear to me that leopards are probably just as fond of water as tigers, and in the hot weather enjoy a cooling swim quite as much. The difference is that they lack the self-confidence of the bigger cats, who, because of their unassailable position in the forest and the animal community, are happy to lie out in mid-river all day, secure in the knowledge that no other creature will attack them in the open.

The monsoon was now approaching again, and I resolved to shift Prince nearer to Tiger Haven, as otherwise he would be cut off from contact with me by the flood waters. I therefore brought him to another platform which I called the Double Storey Machan, and which stood on slightly higher ground only quarter of a mile from the farm.

I had been putting out buffalo-baits for a pair of tigers, and one night, as they wrangled noisily over their kill, the rains broke with unaccustomed violence. Wind howled through the trees, and lightning, thunder and torrents of rain converted the forest into a veritable maelstrom. In a few hours the river surged up and flooded, inundating huge areas; and Prince – obviously alarmed by what was happening all round him – disappeared.

For a week we searched the half-drowned forest in vain, and we had almost given up when one of the farm labourers, hearing a slight sound from across the river, spotted a miserable young leopard perched in the fork of a tree. You and I set off in a boat to the rescue, but before I had even caught sight of him, you gave a bark of recognition, and Prince let out a little chirrup of welcome, evidently delighted that his travails were over. He came down from his tree and greeted us effusively, after which all three of us returned in triumph to the house.

It was now time for you and me to de-camp to Jasbirnagar once more; but before we went I shifted Prince to yet another platform, this time a new one, which I called the Monsoon Machan. The point about this was that it stood on the Escarpment – the line of high ground running roughly east and west behind Tiger Haven – and the site was so much above river level that it could never be flooded.

The snag was that the approach to the machan was long and circuitous: to reach it when the low ground was flooded, I had to drive as far as I could in the jeep, switch to a bicycle and ride along the railway-line, cross two small rivers on rickety bridges and then walk along the Escarpment and down the face to the tree-platform. I went every second day, and usually I found the leopard in residence, but because the journey was so tiresome I never took you with me, and so for several months Prince was deprived of his little companion.

This separation led to a fascinating incident. When the monsoon was tailing off and the waters were receding, you were pregnant with your second family, so I left you at Jasbirnagar as usual and took a son of yours with me to Tiger Haven. The young dog looked so like you as to be almost indistinguishable; but since Prince did not know him, I left him at the farm while I crossed the still-swollen river in a boat to visit the machan.

Having greeted me effusively, the leopard followed me

back to the river. Whether he saw or smelt the dog on the other side, I will never know, but he insisted on hopping into the boat with me, and the moment we touched the opposite bank he sprang ashore and launched himself in pursuit of the dog, who had incautiously come down to the beach to greet us. It was only your son's fleetness of foot that saved him: had he not managed to escape into the house, he would certainly have been killed.

Now, more clearly than ever, I understood that Prince knew you not as a member of the canine species, but as an individual: any other dog – even if it looked exactly like you – was just a dog, to be chased and, if possible, eaten. When the Bible speaks of the lion and the lamb lying down together, one must add the rider that it would have to be a particular lamb.

When the monsoon ended, and the time came for us to return to Tiger Haven, I was apprehensive about what might happen when you and Prince met again after five months apart. I must admit I had been unnerved by the deadly earnest with which the leopard went for your offspring. Would he now remember you, or would he see you, too, as handy prey?

As it happened, he was standing right outside the house as we drew up, looking very large and formidable. You, by contrast, seemed small and fragile, and it was with some trepidation that I let you out of the jeep. I need not have worried: the meeting was so casual that it looked as though you had never been parted: one casual sniff, and off you went together. Your relationship picked up where it had left off, and it only needed the alarm call of a chital to launch the pair of you on a joint pursuit.

Once again I shifted Prince to Leopard Haven, and we continued to visit him there as before. Soon there came another incident which, if I live to be a hundred, I shall never forget.

One evening we arrived to find him stalking a group of a dozen chital stags, together with a fawn. As I called softly to him, he turned his head and gave me a conspiratorial grin, but then continued with his stealthy approach to the deer. You had just taken off to join him in the hunt when suddenly the whole picture changed.

From a nearby tree a langur coughed. Then a swamp-deer barked in warning. I knew at once that some major predator was on the move – and so did every jungle creature within hearing. The chital all called once and bounded off into the tall grass, the white undersides of their raised tails flagging their alarm. Prince turned round and slunk rapidly off in the direction of his headquarters. You came speeding back to me.

A few seconds later the cause of all this panic strolled into view: the resident male tiger, out on his evening rounds, came slowly out of the grass, magnificently silhouetted against a vast, red setting sun. Inevitably the king of the jungle saw me and moved away, but it was a thrilling scene. An unforgettable episode of forest life had unfolded before my eyes, and even you – a domesticated dog – had been part of it, part of the never-ending cycle of life and death. The only stranger, the only jarring element, was myself – an unfamiliar presence whom even the supreme predator had wished to avoid.

By then Prince's fame had begun to spread, and to protect him from the endless stream of visitors who came to see him, I resolved to make him yet another base still further into the forest. I therefore established him on what I named the Ficus Machan (because the platform was built in a ficus or wild fig tree), beyond the river to the north-west. The surrounding area was full of game –

chital, barking deer and wild pig – but its best feature in my eyes was its isolation. The only access to it was by means of a rickety log-bridge which I built over the stream, and the bridge itself was hard to find – so I hoped that no strangers would discover it, and that, if any did, they would fall into the river.

To make Prince feel at home on the new platform, I left him a chital fawn that had been killed by dogs. Next day he had finished it, and you and he celebrated with a joint operation which netted another young deer. His education was proceeding apace – and I was pleased, but not surprised, when, a few weeks later, he made his first kill of an adult animal.

One morning you and I had left him in a tree near the Ficus Machan. When we returned in the evening, and I called to him, a marsh crocodile slid off the bank into the river at the sound of my voice. Prince came across the river on an overhanging branch – rather reluctantly, but safely out of reach of the crocodile underneath – and greeted us in his customary manner – by lifting a paw in languid acknowledgment to you, and honing his body-length against my leg. When I suggested that he should follow us to Leopard Haven for his evening meal, he went back over the river on a bridge of interlaced branches. Presently I heard something heavy being dragged and saw the bushes shaking violently.

Soon Prince re-emerged from the undergrowth, to sit on a sloping branch above the middle of the river, watching me. It was perfectly clear that he wanted me to accompany him, but, not being a monkey, I could not negotiate the sylvan flyover. Instead I sent for Prince's keeper, Ganga Ram, who helped me look after him, and the leopard led the boy to his first major kill – an adult chital hind, which he had despatched in classic leopard fashion by biting it through the throat.

Next morning, when you and I crossed the log bridge, we found the leopard guarding his kill on a small machan which I had put up on some earlier occasion; but except for a small tear in its intestines, the carcase was untouched. Prince was obviously in need of assistance – a fact which he demonstrated by jumping on me repeatedly. I got the carcase disembowelled, which was what he wanted, but was then astonished to see him driven off his own kill by you.

Even knowing your relationship with Prince, I would never have thought such a feat possible, for the leopard was hungry, the kill was his, and you in this instance were no more than an interloper. Yet it was no fluke – for a few minutes later, when we had pulled the carcase across the river to take it to Leopard Haven, you again successfully disputed ownership and became so tremendously possessive that I had to tie you up before Prince was able to drag the prize up to his platform.

Altogether it was an amazing display of will-power – but also of forbearance on the leopard's part, for he would not have tolerated such interference from anyone else. A few days later, when Prince killed a yearling fawn near the Saltlicks below Leopard Haven, he seemed to remember his dispute with you over the previous kill, for he took this one straight up on to his machan. There is no doubt that his association with you hastened his education, teaching him some tricks of his trade that he might have had to learn the hard way if he had been on his own.

The one person in our household who did not care for Prince was my mother. By then old and frail, she naturally felt nervous when the leopard approached her, even if he came with the friendliest intentions; and to give her a comfortable day-time base I built a special circular enclosure of wire-netting, surmounted by a thatched roof, round a jamun tree which stood high above the Junction Pool. Soon the structure was known as Gran's Cage, and in it she would happily knit, play patience or do the crossword while Prince roamed free outside. Sometimes roles were reversed, and we confined Prince in the cage while she took the air outside.

Sometimes you shared the cage with Gran, but your most important function in regard to the old lady was to act as a bodyguard as she walked to and from her place of refuge. So protective of her did you become that you would see off Prince (or the other leopards that followed him) the moment he threatened to annoy her. Although she had tried to get rid of you on the day you arrived, she was by now a great admirer of yours. 'You should write a book about Eelie,' she used to say.

When Prince was twenty-two months old, a team of cameramen and journalists from a young people's magazine called the *Junior Statesman* arrived to collect material for an article about the animal which, on their second visit in April 1973, they termed The Incredible Leopard. I told them they should not underestimate The Incredible Dog, but I do not think they fully appreciated what I meant until they saw you and Prince playing your old game of catch-as-catch-can under the lee of the White Cliffs.

By then he was almost full-grown. He measured six feet eight inches between the pegs – that is, from the tip of his nose to the tip of his tail – and he must have outweighed you about five times; yet he took the greatest care not to injure you. The journalists could hardly believe it when, in the course of your riotous games, the leopard knocked you down and sat on you, but looked the other way as if to avoid the temptation of seizing you by the throat.

About six weeks after that, the event that I had been half hoping for, half dreading, at last occurred. Prince made his break with human mentors, and opted for freedom. On 24 May he twice appeared on the north bank of the river, behind the farm. The first time he sat for half an hour on a fallen tree, gazing across at the house as if fixing it in his memory, before moving off to the east. In the evening he returned, and he called twice as he slowly went past the house in the dusk. Your companion of the past eighteen months – your playmate, pupil and partner – had taken to the wild.

FOUR

Harriet and Juliette

I could not explain to you why I had to leave home in the autumn of 1973, nor did I myself know how long I would be away. I am afraid you must have missed me as much as I missed you, for by then we had got used to spending almost every minute of our lives together. But I believe you trusted me instinctively to return, and for my own part I had the consolation of knowing that you would be well looked after while I was away, either by my staff at Tiger Haven, or by my brother Balram and his wife Mira, who by then were living at Jasbirnagar.

I like to think that I was the most important person in the world to you, just as you were the most important animal to me. But I have to admit that you also became very fond of Kharak Bahadur, a Nepalese servant who took charge of you in my absence. What language you addressed each other in, I am not certain, but you certainly got on very well.

My travels took me first to London, where my book

Tiger Haven was published, and then back to Delhi, where I was fortunate enough to be given a pair of female leopard cubs. For several months before that I had been wondering how I could provide Prince with a mate, and in my anxiety to do my best for him I had written to no less a personage than Mrs Indira Gandhi, then Prime Minister of India, seeking her support in my attempt to help save a threatened species. Her answer was magnificent: she presented me with two orphaned cubs which had been given to her, and which otherwise would have been condemned to a life behind bars in the zoo. I named them Harriet and Juliette, after two attractive girls I had met at a party, and in due course brought them to Tiger Haven.

By that time they were four months old – twice as old as Prince had been when he met you – and although I felt confident that you would know how to deal with them, I could not help worrying that, being a pair, they might gang up on you. For this reason I submitted you to the indignity of living for a couple of days in a large cage while the two cubs roamed at large outside, and I fed all three of you in sight of each other, they outside the enclosure, you in.

On the third day I judged it was time to let you out – and at once I could see that all was going to be well. A three-cornered friendship was quickly established, but the relationship between you and the two sisters was never quite the same as the one you had established with Prince. One obvious difference was that there were two of them, and they relied a good deal on one another for companionship; another, that you were two years older than when Prince had arrived, correspondingly more grown-up, and therefore slightly condescending in your attitude to the newcomers. Thus although you were glad enough to play with them, you had soon had enough of each session, and if they got rough you would snap at them – whereupon they would fall over each other in their efforts to get away from you.

Once you got to know them better, you became keener on these games, and you took to waiting outside their room for them to be released in the morning. As soon as they came out, you would entice them to play by shaking pieces of rope or sacking at them. They in turn would stalk you when they thought you were not looking and try to trip you up by hooking a paw round one of your back legs. But if you happened to glance round and catch them approaching, they would instantly switch their gaze in another direction, as if trying to pretend that they had never had the slightest intention of coming after you.

The longer all four of us shared the same existence, the greater the number of behaviour-differences that continued to emerge. It was clear, for instance, that Harriet and Juliette knew you as an individual, just as Prince had, for when a stray dog appeared at the farm they immediately chased it with murderous intent. In your play, on the other hand, you dominated both young leopards and kept them in order, even though physically smaller than them.

Dominance among animals is generally supposed to relate to body size, and to be determined during play, but other rules obviously obtained in your case, for whereas both leopards would cheerfully leap on to my back, or on to that of each other, once when Juliette sprang at you and found she was going to land on top of you, she instantly adapted her dive so that she came down in a head-roll on the far side of you. Whether she did this to avoid hurting you, or to avert the temptation of making a real, physical attack that landing on top of you might have provoked, I could not be sure; but the incident reminded me very much of the occasion when Prince had sat on you and deliberately looked away. Brought up as I was to regard all animal behaviour as a form of set-piece reaction, I was continually surprised by these subtle variations.

For months we saw nothing of Prince, and during the monsoon of 1973 I lost all trace of him; but in November his familiar pug-marks once again appeared on the approaches to Tiger Haven. By then, I discovered from tracking, he had found a wild mate near Kaima Gaurhi, a cattle station some eight miles to the west, but it seemed that he was being drawn in our direction by the arrival of the two young she-leopards at the farm, even though they were still sub-adult, and not old enough to come into season. How the news reached him, I cannot explain, except to say that it was on some jungle grape-vine not discernible by us degenerate human beings.

Thereafter he paid us intermittent visits, and I had to be extra-careful about protecting you, for although it would have been interesting to see how well he remembered his childhood companion, I was not going to risk you by putting you to the test, especially as Prince had made such a clean break with his past, and I made sure that you slept inside some enclosure every night.

By this time the animal population of Tiger Haven had been boosted by the arrival of three female wolf cubs, brought to me by a young wildlife enthusiast called Nicki Marx. I did not enquire too closely into their origins, for the circumstances of their capture were suspicious, to say the least. Wolves had already been declared a protected species in India, yet these cubs had been given to a friend of mine in Sitapur, a town some seventy-five miles away, by a man who claimed that the local authorities had paid him a reward for killing the mother. The story stank, but it did not surprise me, for corruption is rife throughout India, and it would have been futile to try to find out what had really happened.

I must confess I have a soft spot for wolves, which have been very much maligned – in spite of Kipling's stories about Mowgli, which portray them as excellent characters. The theory that they steal human children gained such wide credence that for generations this fanciful old wives' tale was accepted as a fact by ignorant writers on natural history, and not until 1972, when numbers of wolves had sunk dangerously low, were they placed on the list of endangered species and given protection.

Unfortunately the smallest of the three cubs that came to us soon escaped and vanished forever into the forest, and the other two proved extremely difficult to manage. Nicki tried to win their trust by sleeping in their cage and sitting with them for hours during the day, but the sole result was that they seemed even more scared of him than before, and bolted if they so much as saw him.

The only person who really got through to them was you. Whether you looked on them as wolf-cubs or dog-puppies, I could not be sure, but in any event you adopted them. Again you amazed me by your versatility, for now you somehow understood their special needs and, having gone into their enclosure, you would wait until they put their snouts into the corners of your mouth and then regurgitate food for them – something which a she-wolf would do naturally, but which you had never done for offspring of your own.

Soon they escaped from their cage, and although I managed to get them back in once, they got out again and this time remained at large. Freedom seemed to make them feel easier: they would still not let me touch them, but at least they would come up and sniff my hand. As

Tara and Eelie at Tiger Haven

Tara and Eelie in the jeep ready to set out on a journey

Eelie and Tara watched by Babu Lal

before, it was you who did most to make them fit into the life of the household: you would play the most boisterous games with them, chase them, bowl them over, and bring them to sit with me when I relaxed in the open on summer evenings.

When the leopards began to join in your games, I was worried that in the general excitement one of them might grab a wolf cub and kill it. Again, I had underestimated the capacity of different species to coexist in amity: what should I see one day but Juliette chasing one wolf with the other chasing her!

Anybody out early in the morning that year was liable to witness an amazing sight, for often you, the leopards and the wolves would all come with me when I went for a run along the river bank. I had high hopes that under your tutelage the cubs would adapt fully to life at Tiger Haven, even though the environment was by no means ideal for them, the jungle being utterly different from the open plains which form their natural habitat. But then, with the arrival of the monsoon floods, they simply disappeared, and all your efforts on their behalf were in vain.

All this time my main preoccupation was my attempt to bring up Harriet and Juliette so that I could set them free and establish them in the wild. Naturally there were set-backs, and one occurred in the early summer of 1974, about a year after Prince had left us. One night he came across Harriet just beyond the Junction Bridge, less than a hundred yards from the house, and mauled her, though not seriously. For a while I could not make out what had caused him to attack her. He was certainly not hungry, for he had just passed a young buffalo bait without touching it, and in the end I concluded that he must have been goaded by pique at finding her sexually immature and not responsive to his advances.

Next morning, when you and I went out as usual to see what information fresh tracks would reveal about the night's activities, we found that Prince had gone off past Leopard Haven, pausing to leave scratch-marks on the jamun tree that had been his favourite when he was with us. From Leopard Haven his familiar long stride, with the back feet slightly overlapping the front, led past the pool in the forest that I had named after him and the abandoned Ficus Machan. We both smelt the acrid marking-spray of a leopard – so different from a tiger's pungent squirt – and you had a prolonged sniff at it before you dashed off barking towards some trees in which langurs were giving their tell-tale alarm coughs.

I think both of us had high hopes that contact with our old companion was imminent, when suddenly I saw you hurtling back towards me in great leaps, and there, further off in the open, stood a young tiger, his lean flanks showing that he was probably in search of a meal. As he saw me, he bounded lightly into the long grass at the river's edge. Sad as I was not to have set eyes on Prince, I was thrilled to see how completely in tune you were by then with the forest existence: though you shared a life with me, you had also mastered the lore of the jungle.

Even when the she-leopards completely outstripped you in size, you continued to play rough games with them – but, as when Prince sat on you and looked away, much depended on their forbearance. Some memorable film taken by Dieter Plage, the distinguished cameraman from Survival Anglia Television, shows how Harriet would pull her punches when you rushed in to the attack. She received your charges sitting up on her haunches, yet when she boxed at you with her front paws, she made no attempt to land any blow, but carefully slid one big foot after the other over the top of your head and down the back of your neck.

All went well for nearly another year, but then, in April 1975, tragedy struck, and Juliette, who had never been as robust as her sister, was found poisoned. For me it was a terrible shock, but not altogether unexpected, for local people had always been scared of the leopards, and regarded Tiger Haven as a hotbed of ravening monsters, so I had always been afraid that somebody might try to harm them.

Inevitably this disaster changed the pattern of our existence. Until then, whenever one of the young leopards had come into season, the two sisters had indulged in mock-copulation. With one of them gone, Harriet turned her attention to me, and in self-defence I took to sleeping in the cage recently occupied by the wolf-cubs; and since it was possible that Prince would visit the farm any night, I thought it wise to protect you by having you in the cage with me.

On the night of 15–16 May he paid us just such a visit. I myself slept so soundly that I entirely missed the programme of nocturnal events, but in the morning a mass of tracks showed that there had been an altogether exceptional performance. At some stage in the night Prince had walked confidently over the Junction Bridge and then mated with Harriet for a considerable time within a few yards of the house. Either during or after this session you had got out of our cage through a door which had blown open. Whether the amorous leopards had moved away, whether Prince was not interested in a meal of dog during his mating, or whether he recognised his former companion, I will never know; but in any case you were perfectly safe next morning.

Later in the month tracks again showed that Prince had called on us at night. By then I was sleeping on the open verandah, since Harriet's oestrus cycle had abated for the moment, and you were spending the nights in the wire cage on the back of the jeep. At the time I was aware of nothing except the fact that you gave a few low growls, but in the morning I found that Prince had walked right past my bed.

The last, and most fascinating, encounter between you and Prince took place in November 1975. Again, I was scarcely aware of his visit, but next morning the evidence of it was unmistakably printed in the heavy dew on the concrete floor of the verandah outside the dining-cum-drawing-room.

As usual he approached over the Junction Bridge, then jumped up on to the three-foot high plinth of the verandah and walked along the length of my bed. I believe that he rubbed himself against it, as he used to do when he was living with me, for I remember becoming vaguely aware of a slight tremor about midnight. Unfortunately I was too sleepy, and too well wrapped up against the winter cold, to bother to look out. In any case, he went round the end of the bed and stood with his face to the wire screen on the drawing-room door, inside which I had put you to bed. What his intentions were will never be known: he may simply have been hungry, but I like to believe that there is good in nature, and I thought at the time that he had come to pay one final visit to his childhood companion. Now, looking back, I feel almost sure of it, for my experience with tigers has shown me that the great cats have far greater powers of memory and recognition than is generally recognised. I am almost sure that when Prince stood at the drawing-room door he was saying goodbye.

After that, so far as I am aware, you never met Prince again. For many more months you and I were closely involved with the leopards, and Prince mated twice more with Harriet, but both encounters took place in the forest, out of your immediate ken.

When Harriet became pregnant, your attitude towards her underwent a significant alteration. You had no intellectual means of knowing why she was suddenly different, yet it was clear to me that with your subtle animal instincts you sensed the biological and chemical changes taking place in her body, for you treated her more gently and with greater deference than before. It was as if you wanted to give her all the help you could by not imposing on her at a difficult time.

Unfortunately you did not see much of Harriet's first family – two cubs whose lives proved wretchedly short. They were born in April 1977 on a machan which I had specially built as a maternity ward. Soon, however, their mother shifted them down to ground level, and when the monsoon floods rose, in an astonishing display of trust she brought them to the safety of Tiger Haven – little balls of grey fluff spotted with black – carrying them by the scruff of the neck, one at a time, into an upstairs room, only just ahead of the rising waters.

After a week she became restive and demanded a lift over the still-swollen river by jumping into the boat. I dutifully ferried her across, taking one cub on each journey, and she established the family in a narrow ravine, where a den under the roots of a tree gave them a secure base. Alas for all her efforts, and for mine: at the end of July, when the cubs were exactly three months old, one was killed by a tigress whose own offspring had been trampled to death by elephants, and the other was accidentally drowned as Harriet tried to bring it across the river.

It was another grievous setback. As luck would have it, I was again in England at the time, and heard the news there. My one consolation was that I had already set out on another and still more ambitious voyage of wildlife exploration.

FIVE

Likes and Dislikes

I should do you an injustice, and also distort the truth, if I tried to pretend that you were as obsessed with wild life as I was. Perhaps the most remarkable thing about you was that you so easily led a double life: when in the forest you behaved with the instincts and reactions of a wild animal, but in the house and around the farm you were just like any domesticated dog.

Driving, for instance, was a favourite hobby, and you always loved going for rides in the jeep, whether your companions were human or feline or both; but you also developed a dangerous habit, which annoyed me very much, of jumping out of the window whenever you spotted something worth chasing, even if the vehicle was on the move.

In the business of ratting, there was no one to touch you: field rats were your speciality, and your record bag was twenty-six in a single day, all caught as rising water flushed them out of the banks in a paddy field. Sometimes a rat would get into the house, and there too your ability was extraordinary. If you detected a potential victim behind the book-case in the drawing-room, you would meticulously pull out the books, one by one, with your teeth, by no means improving them, and all of us humans would join in the hunt to prevent the library being ruined, for not until your jaws had closed on the quarry would you lay off.

Your strong sense of property led you to guard the house against outsiders with the greatest enthusiasm: you hated strangers, particularly if they were unkempt or ill-dressed, and a dhoti, or loin cloth, aroused your special wrath. Anybody wearing one was sure to be bitten about the ankles – and the more I tried to stop you, the more persistent you became, circling around to keep out of reach, and pressing home one quick attack after another. Even the bona fide tourists who came to stay in the winter months you treated with disdain.

One local to whom you took special exception was the honey-collector, who raided the bees' nests high in the trees of the forest. Admittedly he was always dressed in rags, but he was an intrepid fellow, prepared to climb acrobatically and take on the bees without any form of protective clothing, so it seemed a bit tough that you should go for him when he was bringing me honey!

You were still more aggressive whenever you came with me to round up graziers who had illegally taken their cattle to graze inside the boundaries of the Dudhwa National Park, which is a sanctuary reserved for wildlife. I am convinced that these trespassers were more frightened of you than of me, for although I used to set about them physically (that being the only language that had any effect), I always pulled my punches. You, on the other hand, had no inhibitions. I remember one particular instance most vividly. I had got hold of a cowherd and started slapping his face. At first he did not seem much put out by my gentle blows; then he started hopping about in an agitated way, and when I looked down I saw that you were busily engaged in taking chunks out of his bare legs. Word went round like lightning that the sahib's small dog was a terror, and thereafter whenever an intruder saw us approaching together, he would shin up a tree like a monkey.

In all the years we were together, I never remember you being ill. No doubt such robust health owed much to proper feeding – you always had one meal a day, generally of cooked meat, in the evening – but I am sure your own good sense played a part in it, for you were never greedy, and never scrounged for tit-bits. Sometimes in the forest you would pinch a bit of raw meat from some wild predator's carcase, but this was generally a tactical move, designed to establish your rights, rather than a sign of hunger. The same was true of your evening skirmishes with the elephants. Often you were present when Bhagwan Piari and Sitara were brought by their *filwans*, or keepers, to the front of the house, where, as a little ritual, I would give them their evening ration of four thick barley cakes apiece, known as *roti*. Compared with your own, the elephants' rations were singularly unappetising – a kind of unleavened bread, with a good deal of black salt in it – nevertheless, you would sometimes decide you would like some too and demonstrate noisily, barking so loudly that the pachyderms began to shuffle about uneasily. Had you not been restrained on a leash, I am sure you would have taken possession of the food – even though your own weight of about thirty pounds was pitted against a combined aggregate of twenty thousand pounds – just for the satisfaction of asserting yourself. Obviously the proverbial dog in the manger was similarly motivated.

In general, you were extremely popular with all members of my household, not least my mother, who, after her initial opposition had become devoted to you. At the very end of her life, as she lay ill in bed, I offered to bring you to visit her, because I thought it would cheer her up. She said – no, thank you. She would rather Eelie did not see her in such a low state. All the same, I brought you, and I was very much moved when I found that you would not leave the room. Somehow you knew that the old lady was dying, and you refused to abandon her. A few days later, after her death, her body was brought back to the farm for the night before her cremation, as is the custom in our part of India, and again in some mysterious way you felt you must go to her aid: unnoticed by anyone else, you slipped into the room where the coffin was lying and spent the night there.

The one member of our establishment with whom you did not see eye to eye was Abou Bakr, the goat. Your distaste, I must admit, was not entirely ill-founded, for although certainly a character in his own right, and a creature of undoubted courage, he was never the most attractive animal to have around. (His name, based on the Hindustani word *bakra*, meaning he-goat, had derisive connotations.)

I got him originally as a bait for Prince, after the leopard had taken to the wild. In the old days of sport-shooting a goat was the favourite bait for leopards: its bleating would draw intended victims to the spot in the forest where the hunter waited in ambush on a camouflaged machan. I am sorry to say I got Abou Bakr for much the same purpose, hoping he would help me locate Prince.

The goat, however, through a combination of good luck and the possession of a temperament that gave him no urge to bleat, even when left alone in the jungle, escaped the attentions of both Prince and Harriet. In his early days he would give one or two perfunctory cries, but later, with his natural stoicism fortified by experience, he would simply curl up and go to sleep. Even his phenomenal smell somehow failed to penetrate the jungle fastnesses.

Thus he survived. I decided to reprieve him, and he became a permanent fixture at the farm, where, to your considerable disgust, he attempted to lord it over all the other inhabitants. The most immediately offensive thing about him was his smell, which he constantly intensified by his charming habit of urinating on his own head. But the main trouble was his aggressive response to friendly overtures: though essentially a sociable animal, he became deeply frustrated by the lack of female company, and tried to ease his feelings by accosting everyone he came across. He would approach humans of either sex with throaty cries of passion, which provoked much ribald laughter from bystanders; and even full-grown buffaloes, though infinitely larger, did not escape his attention: whenever one of them failed to respond appropriately to his advances, he would engage him in physical combat – a habit which cost him a broken horn. It was small wonder that you never had any time for him.

Yet, even with Abou Bakr's noisome presence, our community at Tiger Haven was a happy one, and I knew that I would be taking no small risk by bringing into it a member of the species which dominates all others in the jungle – *Panthera tigris tigris*, the Indian tiger.

SIX

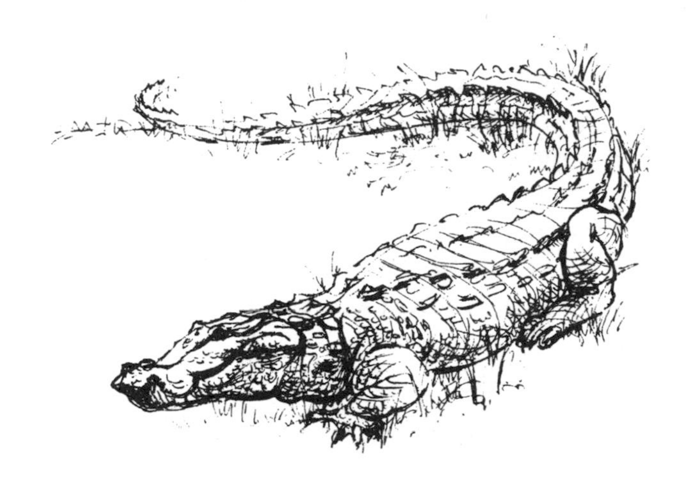

Tiger in the House

You never knew how lucky you were to have been spared the bureaucracy which bedevilled my attempt to import a tiger cub from England and set it free in the forest. The project appeared to have everything in favour of it, including the support of our Prime Minister, Mrs Gandhi; for by that date the Indian Government had committed itself to rescuing tigers from oblivion. Surveys made in the early 1970s had revealed that the entire wild population – once measured in hundreds of thousands – was now no more than 1,800; and in 1972 India had launched Project Tiger, an all-out attempt to save the species.

Naturally I felt that it would help if I showed it was possible to return a zoo-born tiger to the wild, thereby increasing stocks by at least one head. But at every stage of my attempt to import the cub, there were Indian officials ready to block it if they could.

There is no need to recount all the obstruction here.

Suffice it to say that late in September 1976 I eventually reached Tiger Haven at the end of a tiresome journey, bringing with me a four-month-old female cub called Tara, whom I had collected from Twycross Zoo in Leicestershire. Because the monsoon had not yet finished, and the approaches to the farm were still waterlogged, the young tigress had to complete the last stretch of her journey on elephant-back.

The idea of introducing Tara to you did not alarm me much: I felt sure your experience with the leopards would stand you in good stead. The animal whose possible reaction worried me most was Harriet: having just lost her own cubs to a tigress, she could hardly be expected to welcome another member of that dangerous species into her foster-home. I therefore took such precautions as I could, and proceeded carefully.

You were the first member of the household to greet us. We picked you up at Jasbirnagar, and you rode beside me in the front of the jeep as far as the Ghulli Bridge, where the track to Tiger Haven leaves the main road. There we loaded the tigress, in her crate, on to Sitara's back.

Fortunately, before my trip to London, I had had the drawing-room verandah enclosed with wire mesh, so that it formed a useful cage, and into this I put Tara, wearing a collar, for the first two days. You, roaming about outside, and being fed in sight of her, showed intense curiosity over the striped newcomer, but never the slightest sign of fear, and your reaction made a striking contrast with that of another dog which Tara and I had come across in London. There a Jack Russell terrier belonging to Colin Willock, Executive Director of Survival Anglia Television, was plainly terrified of the tiger cub and avoided the stable in which she had been housed for a whole fortnight.

At first I was at a loss to see how a terrier, born and bred in London, could know what the baby tiger was, or what a formidable animal she would grow into. Then I remembered how at Jasbirnagar a langur had barked in alarm at the sight of the infant Prince arriving – even though the monkey, which lived some distance from the forest, had never seen a leopard in its life; and I reflected again on the fineness of an animal's intuitive perception. Your calm reaction, on the other hand, was clearly conditioned by the five years you had spent with leopards, and by all your experience in the jungle.

In any event, on the third day we took you and Tara out for a walk together, both on leashes. On the fifth day we let Tara go and waited tensely. Big cat and small dog sniffed each other carefully. You, I must say, seemed almost excessively casual. Then the tigress, unable to restrain her exuberance any longer, leapt on you. At once you retaliated by baring your fangs and giving her a couple of nips: this immediately established the order of precedence and settled the basis of your relationship. Even though Tara soon outgrew you, you could always dominate her if you wanted. When you did give her a nip, she would lie down and bawl.

There now remained the much more delicate task of introducing Tara to Harriet. On the day we reached Tiger Haven the leopard was in a tree on the other side of the river, so I sent the boat across to fetch her. She hopped into it readily enough, but then immediately sensed that something was abnormal, and her face assumed a tense, hunted look. The moment she landed, she rushed up a tree and stayed there gazing at the cage where Tara was enclosed but invisible. Her acute intuition warned her that there on the verandah was a member of the species which had caused the death of her own cubs and greatly inhibited her wanderings in the forest. Half-an-hour later she came down and sat in the boat, but when she found that no one was prepared to row her over the river, she swam across on her own.

After refusing food for a couple of days, she gradually recovered her usual appetite and began to spend more time at Tiger Haven. I fed her outside Tara's cage, and the revulsion which she had displayed at first changed to apparent indifference.

On the tenth day, with you standing by as a mutual acquaintance and an insurance of goodwill, I let Tara loose in Harriet's presence. As soon as the leopard realised that there were no bars between them, she raced up a tree, but immediately came down, ran at Tara and roared at her. Tara rolled over and grinned submissively, but roared defensively when she felt crowded. Then Harriet, apparently sensing that this was only a cub, started trying to play with her. Tara, however, was nervous, and when the leopard crept up and ran at her, she inclined her head with an ingratiating snarl and rolled over with another defensive roar as Harriet leapt lightly over her.

As all this went on, you ran from one animal to the other, reassuring both of them, as befitted someone of your unbiased position and mature status. I myself heaved a sigh of relief, for Harriet had not been collared for some time, and it would have been difficult to take the two animals out together if they had not got on well.

Soon I started leading group walks through the forest every morning and evening. In the past, when you and I went out on such excursions, Harriet had not shown much interest in coming with us; but now she suddenly tagged along, and it was clear that the cause of her change of heart was Tara.

We made a pretty mixed procession – myself in the lead, followed by you, Tara and Harriet, usually in that order but sometimes switching as one cat tried to ambush the other. Tara was normally the instigator of these games, but she was still nervous of Harriet, and if the leopard happened to look round as she was creeping up, she would stop and pretend that nothing had been further from her mind than an attack on her spotted playmate.

Your role was that of mediator: you would gambol back and forth from one companion to the other, and it was perfectly clear to me that your influence as a catalyst between the wild world of the major carnivores and the domestic world of man had been a decisive factor in getting this unnatural friendship forged so smoothly. You were the honest broker – the compassionate, modulating force which tempered the reactions of these heavily-armed cats towards each other. Without your calming presence, their meeting might well have been explosive, possibly lethal.

Our walks continued in this uninhibited fashion, with Tara the most boisterous member of the party. As everyone got to know each other better, I saw that you and Harriet looked upon the little tigress as a wayward juvenile whose pranks had to be tolerated and even, within limits, encouraged. One day on our return to the farm we all sat down for a breather, but the interlude evidently seemed rather pointless to Tara, who promptly jumped on you. Finding herself rebuffed, she tried to climb on my head, but Harriet, who was sitting close by, ran at her and spanked her.

Soon Harriet started making friendly advances to Tara, and the way that she would go and sit near her, whenever the tigress's restless temperament allowed it, suggested that she was being impelled by some inner motivation. Her own cubs, had they lived, would have been only ten days older than Tara, and it seemed possible that Harriet's maternal instinct was now somehow making her associate this oversized infant with her own lost offspring. The same maternal possessiveness which had driven the Big Tigress to pursue the leopard cubs after the death of her own now seemed to be driving Harriet to accept the offspring of another cat genus. It was an illuminating quirk of behaviour, but I doubt if she would have reacted so positively if the new cub had been a jackal or a wolf.

Sometimes Harriet tried to persuade Tara to follow her into the forest, and later she encouraged her to chase her up trees, by going up a certain distance and looking back to see whether or not she was following. Tara's clumsy attempts at climbing made a ludicrous contrast with the fluid movements of the leopard, and she confirmed my belief that although young tigers *can* climb, they are essentially terrestrial animals and prefer being on the ground. The perpendicular teak tree which Harriet would ascend in stages was too much for Tara, and she never got beyond a certain height, even though I tried to tempt her with pieces of sacking held just beyond her reach. The difference between the two animals was fascinating to observe: a leopard can cling to the bark of a vertical tree-trunk with its claws, stay motionless, and then propel itself upwards by sheer muscular strength. A tiger, in spite of the colossal power in its limbs, cannot do this; nor does it have an inherited instinct to climb.

Nevertheless, Tara provided one striking illustration of how far an animal can adapt its basic nature. Once, when hunting in tandem with you, she caught a fawn, and instead of eating it on the ground, as a tiger normally would, she took it up a tree to keep it out of your reach, thus inflicting on you exactly the same frustration as you had endured with Prince. Admittedly the tree had a sloping trunk, and was an easy climb, but she would

Billy with Harriet and Eelie

Tara pushing Eelie down a bank

Eelie and Tara playing in the ploughed field at Tiger Haven

never have taken her kill up it at all if it had not been for the element of competition introduced by your presence.

Our walks were the most important part of the acclimatisation process which I had planned for Tara, and they usually lasted two hours. Under your persuasive influence Tara and Harriet gradually became easier with one another, but it was fascinating to see how finely each of you judged the extent of the liberties that might be taken by one of the others.

Once, for instance, Tara ran at you, knocked you down and playfully grabbed your throat, no doubt as an instinctive try-out of the tactics which she would have to use in later life to kill prey and feed herself. You lay there inert, but I was never for a moment worried, as I could see that the whole thing was play. Up came Harriet: as she sniffed Tara's neck, you still lay quiet, but when she jumped on top of the heap, you, the underdog, decided this was too much, and wriggled out from your lowly position to rout first the leopard and then the tigress.

In spite of her efforts to be friendly, Harriet was always careful to keep physical contact to a minimum, instinctively cutting down the chance of an aggressive encounter, which is always likely among the solitary cats, with their volatile temperament and formidable armament. You, however, had no such inhibitions, which was why your personality proved such a positive factor in the tricky process of introduction.

Before the monsoon floods abated, pools and stretches of water lay everywhere, and, with the weather still so hot and steamy, Tara would wallow in every one we came to along our way. Just like you – and indeed all the animals I have kept – she preferred drinking the rich mineral water in mud-holes to the sweet water which I provided. Altogether, water was an important element in Tara's life. One day we drove by jeep to Kawaghatia, to the west of Tiger Haven, taking Mike Price, one of Survival Anglia's cameramen. For most of the six-mile return journey you and Tara played enchantingly, chasing each other, in clouds of spray, in and out of the pools by the river. Alas, the film got ruined in processing, so that posterity was deprived of a unique spectacle.

Gradually I extended our walks, leading the way along jungle paths so as to familiarise Tara with the immediate range round Tiger Haven. Our excursions would also serve notice on the resident Big Tigress that a newcomer had arrived on her territory. Soon I estimated that we had established a range of about fifteen square miles – a fact of vital importance to both cats, but of only academic interest to you, even though by then, through so much association with members of the species, you had practically become an honorary cat yourself.

Inevitably, as Tara grew up and Harriet began coming into season again, life grew more serious and difficult. One night I heard the leopard wrangling in renewed courtship with Prince, and when she appeared in the morning, she had a cut angling across her nose, as if he had swiped her for refusing to go with him. Naturally she was not in the best of tempers, but she greeted you in the normal way with a lift of one front paw, and, after getting a dab of iodine on her cut, was ready enough to come walking. All went well until, with great perversity, you and Tara decided to ambush her – whereupon she struck back sharply, knocking the tigress down and biting her, and swiping you as well.

When we started to extend our range north of the river, we would all cross over together in the boat. Each short voyage was quite a performance, for the boat was very crowded and both cats were restless when afloat. In her eagerness to reach the other shore Tara would lean her whole weight – already perhaps a hundred and fifty pounds – against the man in the bow, and threaten to overturn the entire party. The one animal who remained composed and quiet during the crossings was yourself.

On New Year's Day Tara celebrated by spraying for the first time on an electricity pylon which stood outside her night cage. Next you came up, sniffed the spray mark and solemnly did a token urination. It was then Harriet's turn to plant her own spray beneath that of the tigress. This became more or less standard routine: as we moved through the forest, tiger, dog and leopard ritually anointed many a favourite tree, and I concluded that the process was one more method of demonstrating your increasing familiarity with each other.

Though Tara was growing fast, and was already much bigger than Harriet, you and the leopard both still treated her as a juvenile, and tolerated her wayward behaviour as though she were a boisterous child. But in spite of her occasional foolishness the tigress already displayed a fine power of discrimination in her sense of smell, becoming much more agitated if she detected the spray of a male tiger rather than that of a female. You, on the other hand, seemed not to worry what sort of tiger had left the deposit. You were obviously capable of distinguishing between Tara's spray and that of other tigers, but you seemed to find my presence so reassuring that the prospect of a chance encounter with another big cat did not bother you.

Soon Tara outgrew the cage built into the back of the jeep, so I took to going for tandem drives with you sitting beside me in the front seat, Harriet in the back, and the tigress in another cage on a trailer. Once a herd of about two hundred swamp-deer, or barasingha, suddenly came into view. The moment I released Tara, she gave chase, and a magnificent scene ensued. Clouds of dust rose from eight hundred thundering hooves as the deer charged round and round in the tall grass, and from the melée came the falsetto shrieks of the does and immature males, counterpointed by the deep, booming bass of the big antlered stags. In spite of their alarm calls, the deer seemed to enjoy the performance as much as Tara did, and certainly as they galloped in circles the chase made a marvellous merry-go-round of predator and prey.

A tiger's normal method of hunting is to stalk its prey to within close range, and then spring on it with a short, fast charge. Tara's habit of galloping hopefully after deer was so much more dog-like than cat-like that for a while I thought she must have picked it up from you. Then I realised that she was not so much imitating you as being triggered into sudden action by seeing you take off; and sure enough, as she grew older, her true cat instincts asserted themselves, so that she stopped wildly chasing and began to stalk instead.

By the time she was a year old, Tara had grown her permanent set of teeth. I was interested to see that the old canines did not drop out to make way for the new ones, but moved off to either side and fell out only when they had been replaced. This, I concluded, was nature's way of ensuring that a big cat is never deprived of its essential equipment. For you, the practical result was not so good, for Tara could now splinter the pig-bones which until then she had only been able to gnaw, and she herself cleaned up the marrow, which before had been shared around. You were forced to rely on left-overs from Harriet, who was often away in the forest on her own affairs.

SEVEN

More Adventures

In northern India the hot season, before the outbreak of the monsoon, lasts from mid-April to mid-June. During these two months westerly winds, as searing and desiccating as if they blew out of a furnace, blast the parched grasslands and exhaust men and animals alike. And yet this season, debilitating though it can be, has a peculiar fascination.

Great thunderheads start to build up over the Nepal hills, which on clear days gleam faintly like giant white teeth on the horizon far to the north. As occasional rainstorms sweep down over the forests, the winds whirl sal seeds from the top of the Escarpment like the myriad miniature parachutes of an invading Lilliputian army, and sometimes the illusion is intensified by a barrage of hailstones. Scorching days are followed by cool nights, which provide respite for a faltering world.

Only the river valley retains its freshness: protected by the tall sal and jamun trees, whose perennial foliage is renewed by young yellow-and-green leaves as the old ones fall, the stream meanders through dense woodlands and savannah, and all wildlife concentrates along its luscious green belt. Here the tiger sits in the water to cool off, his head hardly showing among the fallen tree-trunks, washed down by last year's floods, which lie in the stream like sunken battleships, with their upturned roots waving as though they were tentacles of Medusa's hair. Here the prey animals come down to drink, until strident alarm-calls trigger a stampede to safer ground. At night the grazing ungulates crop the short grasses of the meadow and rest out in the open as a precaution against prowling predators. The rhythm of life and death continues. There is no heaven or hell for animals, except those created by man.

As the hot weather set in again, you and Tara played more and more in the river. To an outsider the games looked thoroughly alarming, for the tigress was already six or seven times your weight, and it seemed as though you must be crushed. But size was not everything: although often chased yourself, it was frequently you who did the chasing – and Tara treated you with special care and gentleness. Thus although she would jump right onto my back and knock me down, and try to wrestle me into the water if she found herself above me on the river bank, she would never actually jump onto you, but would make sure that she swerved off in the final instant of a charge.

By the time the rains broke, at the end of June, Harriet was about to give birth again, and she spent the last night of her pregnancy in an upstairs room at Tiger Haven. Overnight the river was transformed from a torpid, translucent stream into a torrent of liquid mud, and there now occurred the local phenomenon known as

'Uchchowa', in which the river fish die by the thousand, their gills choked with silt. As the river falls – which happens very fast, as the flood waters are soaked up by the parched earth – the gasping fish are left stranded, to rot in the heat of the sun, now blazing from a rain-washed sky. Predators have a bonanza: Brahminy kites wheel and swoop, pond herons sit contentedly on the bank, and the otters no longer have to contend for spoils. But nature's scavengers cannot clean up the bounty fast enough, and soon an ever-increasing stench pollutes the banks as the remaining fish putrefy.

You had already witnessed this strange event six or seven times, but still you were interested by it, and I remember how one day you went up to a pile of rotting fish and wrinkled your nose as if to signify that it was a bit much, even for you. In exactly the same way, a few days later, Tara went up to Jackson, my tracker, and wrinkled her face in the tiger grimace known as *Flehmen*, showing that his sweat-drenched clothes and unwashed body exuded a no less remarkable odour. (I should explain that my tracker was an Indian, his real name was Charan, but someone once pointed out his amazing resemblance to Beatrix Potter's toad, Mr Jackson, and the name stuck.)

Now that the floods were up, the only means of reaching the dry ground on the Escarpment was by boating across the swollen river, and Tara unfortunately had her own ideas about how this should be accomplished. After trying to wrestle me and my assistant Babu Lal into the water, she would pretend she was not interested in the expedition, but once the humans had boarded the boat, she would take a flying leap into the middle of it, almost capsizing the craft. You, clearly realising that it was safest to keep out of the way until the last moment, would wait until we were ready. Then at my coaxing you would step down amidships and sit stolidly on the floorboards until we reached the other side, ignoring Tara's overtures to have a game in mid-stream. The tigress, getting no rise out of you, would pace restlessly up and down the boat in her haste to reach the far bank, leaning her two-hundred-pound bulk against the man paddling in the bow. This habit could easily have landed one of us in the swirling waters, so we took it in turns to paddle, and the person being leant on concentrated on clinging to the gunwale. As we drew in to the other shore Tara would leap out on to the bank and rush up the Escarpment. If Harriet was with us, she would be the next to disembark, and only after everyone else had gone ashore could you be induced to step out of the boat.

Our walks north of the river often took us along the earth roads of the Dudhwa National Park, and there we inevitably sometimes met other people. One of our most memorable encounters was with Khalid, the gate-keeper of the Park, on his way to the forest station at Sathiana. He came round a corner suddenly, pushing a bicycle, and I saw him too late to divert him through the undergrowth, away from our animals. At that moment you happened to be excavating an anthill, and Tara was busy investigating a bush beside the road. As Babu Lal placed himself squarely in front of her, I told Khalid to walk on slowly down the road. All went well until he came level with Tara. The sight of her so close was too much for him: his nerve broke, he leapt on to his machine, and pedalled off furiously.

The sudden movement was too much for *you* as well. No doubt thinking that your companions, hitherto so dull, had at last decided to liven up the expedition, you and Tara took off in pursuit, with you in the lead. The pair of you were decidedly faster than Khalid, and a crescendo of terrified yells echoed off into the forest as he rode frantically down the road. In the end he fell off into an outcrop of bushes, whereupon you and the tigress, disappointed at the premature end of what had promised to be an enjoyable chase, came back to your normal companions. When he got home Khalid wrote a lavishly-worded complaint to the Chief Wildlife Warden, offering to resign.

In our acclimatisation programme we were much harassed by the Big Tigress, who had had another litter of cubs, and clearly regarded Tara as an interloper on her range. One morning when I happened to be away Babu Lal took you and the tigress for your usual walk; on the way back he noticed that you both seemed uneasy, and when he looked round he saw the Big Tigress following the party. He shouted at her, and she disappeared into the bushes, only to pop out again a moment later. Ignoring further yells, she followed persistently. But Tara, after becoming very nervous, seemed to gain confidence as you drew near home, and when you reached the river she sat in the water as usual, with Babu Lal sitting on the bank and you in between.

Suddenly Tara stood up, looked towards Babu Lal and gave a nervous *Prusten* – the fluttering of the lips which tigers use for greeting. Turning, he found the Big Tigress scarcely ten yards behind him; but luckily when she saw that she was observed, she turned and bounded lightly away.

Going to investigate the next day, I found from pug-marks that the tigress was being accompanied by a single cub about five months old. Again she followed us, but she went off when we turned towards her, and neither you nor Tara seemed in the least scared. But that was not the end of the day's excitement.

We were nearly back to the Escarpment Machan when Tara, who was in the lead, suddenly went into a crouch opposite some dense bushes, and flattened herself on the ground at right-angles to the path. I was about ten yards behind, followed by you and Jackson, who had a tin can full of stones so that he could set up a loud rattle if we needed to scare any animal off.

In front of Tara's nose the dense bushes were being agitated as some animal pushed its way out towards the path. Tara began to quiver with excitement, raising her rump and swaying from side to side to maintain balance for an attack. Tension mounted as the agitation in the bushes came closer. First I glimpsed something black, and then the off-white snout of a large sloth bear, which seemed, from the angle at which I was looking, only a few inches from Tara's nose.

The bear half rose into a defensive stance on his hind legs, changed his mind, decided on attack, and with a roar launched himself at the tigress. Tara fled down the path, straight towards me, closely pursued by the infuriated bear, who looked like a runaway tank, his black bulk overflowing the path to right and left. I waved my stick and shouted. Jackson beat on his tin can. I just had time to wonder what would happen if the incensed creature arrived in our midst when he gave a guttural bark and veered off at right-angles into the undergrowth.

You, who had missed the initial excitement, launched fearlessly into pursuit. Tara took off after you. There was a terrific crashing through the bushes, and the bear, under pressure, gave another bark. It was not long before you came back with a satisfied expression on your face; but Tara, perhaps because her dignity had been ruffled by her own ignominious flight, continued the chase a bit longer. The cause of the bear's quick temper was easy to discern: as he turned off the path, I saw that the skin on his rump was bare, red and angry with mange. (A year later, when Jackson came on him again, he had fully recovered, and reacted more calmly.)

Another animal which gave you and Tara a good deal to think about was a porcupine that you flushed out of some grass. The big rodent, weighing perhaps thirty pounds, had climbed a sloping tree-trunk, partly to get out of the rising flood-waters and partly to evade the other animals which it must have heard approaching. Tara charged into the water, caught the porcupine by the head and flicked it onto dry land, where it lay still alive but obviously injured. The tigress, not sure what to do next, sat with her paw on it. When I called her, she came out of the water with a quill stuck in her throat. After I had removed it, she returned to the porcupine and would not leave it.

In the afternoon, when we returned to the scene, the tableau was exactly the same: still she sat there, with her paw on the still-living animal and a frown on her brow. Then she came padding through the water and hooked a paw round my leg, asking for help. As dark was falling, the most humane thing seemed to be to kill the injured animal. This we did, and after we had skinned it, we gave it to Tara to eat – except for a small portion which we cooked for the other actress in the drama.

As the weeks went by, Tara's hunting became more professional, although she was still influenced by you and your habit of hurtling in pursuit of anything that moved. Her forest-sense was also steadily improving, but even now our steps were dogged by the Big Tigress, who was gunning for Tara with ever-increasing zeal in instinctive protection of her own family. Finally she launched a full-scale attack.

One morning, on my way back from a wildlife meeting

in Lucknow, I got an extraordinary telepathic intimation of disaster. I was staying the night with friends at Lakhimpur, some fifty miles from Tiger Haven, and at 5 a.m. I awoke sweating from a nightmare in which I had heard distress roars from Tara, and although you, Harriet and I ran towards them as fast as we could, the calls kept getting further away. At the time I thought no more about the dream, but that evening, when I eventually reached home after a journey made difficult by the floods, I found that somehow I had picked up vibrations of a real event. Tara *had* been attacked by the Big Tigress, and had sustained wounds severe enough to need treatment; but luckily, thanks to the strong nerves and skill of the vet who came and gave her a sedative, and anti-tetanus and antibiotic injections, she soon recovered.

EIGHT

Tara Chooses Freedom

I hope I have shown what an indispensable role you played in Tara's education. As time went on, however, the bonds between you inevitably weakened. There were three main reasons. First, Tara kept growing, so that the physical disparity between you became ever more marked. Second, you yourself were getting older and less agile, so that your relish for rough games naturally diminished. But the third and main reason was that the tigress was becoming steadily more independent and less reliant on the companions who had brought her up.

When the cooler weather came round again, she became more playful for a while; but now her attitude to you had undergone another subtle change. Sometimes during our forest walks she would stand next to you with her ears turned back, as if thinking it rather strange that so puny a creature should be there beside her, and wondering how your relationship had come about.

Against her great bulk you looked positively frail – yet even now, if need be, you would set about her with shrill yelps and drive her off. Whenever she started wrestling with me, for instance, you would immediately take my side and chase her off, resenting the excessive familiarity.

The closeness of your friendship with the tiger was demonstrated by a remarkable incident which took place at the farm. A fat businessman with a strong interest in wildlife had got into the habit of paying us visits, and one day was sitting on a tree-stump outside the house when Tara appeared. For some reason she took against the newcomer, who was wielding a fancy camera, and knocked him off his perch. As he picked himself up, full of sudden anger and fright, he launched a kick at the tigress – whereupon you, instantly siding with your big cat companion, rushed at him and bit him in the ankle.

As winter drew on we found it more and more difficult to shut Tara into her night cage. One afternoon you went off with her on a typical freelance expedition, chasing deer at the edge of a ploughed field, but although you yourself came back at nightfall, she did not. After dark chital began calling frantically in the open field, and when I switched on the jeep's searchlight, its beam lit up a mass of eyes – numerous small eyes of deer close at hand, and further off a single pair infinitely more luminous, changing colour with every alteration of angle from light green to smouldering red and the white-hot radiance of a powerful electric bulb. The chital were galloping in a circle uttering a chorus of girlish yelps, and Tara was bounding after them with frequent pauses to regain her breath.

When Babu Lal and I got into the jeep, you insisted on coming with us. Out in the field, fantastic shadows lengthened and shortened as animals swept across our advancing lights until in the end the tempo of the chase slackened. Finally, blinded by the glare, Tara walked up to us with a *Prusten*, and Babu Lal slipped a noose round her neck.

In November that year you performed perhaps one of your most remarkable feats. Tara was then eighteen months old and well on the way to independence. After our morning walk she went off into the copse beyond the Junction Bridge to spend the day (as I thought) in a patch of grass. At three in the afternoon I suddenly heard loud distress calls. Though almost certain they came from some species of deer, I was still obsessed about the threat from the Big Tigress, and so I ran towards them as fast as I could.

On the way you overtook me, going like a bullet to investigate. The cries were coming from the patch of grass, and you shot into it ahead of me. A few moments later I came on a sambhar fawn cowering in the narrow stream of the Soheli, where it had sought to take refuge. Tara had hold of it by the rump and was trying to drag it up on to higher ground.

I hurried back to cross the river by the bridge, so that I could get a better view of events. The next thing I saw was the astounding spectacle of one small dog standing in mid-stream and nipping at the fawn, which was bigger than you. The tigress, whom you had driven off her legitimate kill, was running up and down the bank in frustration. Amazed as I was by your achievement, I felt that Tara must have what belonged to her; but it was not until I had taken you home and tied you up there that she went back into the water to pull her kill on to dry land.

To keep other tigers off, I surrounded the dead fawn with a protective barrier of white cloth, hitched to bushes and clumps of grass, which is generally enough to scare casual prowlers away. Tara stayed at the scene of her triumph, and by next morning had bitten off the tail and eaten one hind leg, as well as part of the other, in the conventional manner of feeding tigers. When we visited her at the scene, she was very friendly, but because I felt certain that you would launch another attempt to claim the kill, I kept you on a lead. Sure enough, you made a spirited effort to get within striking distance, but I held on to you. As you were certainly not hungry, I could only conclude that it was once again the proverbial dog-in-the-manger instinct that had been driving you on.

Tara moved steadily on towards full independence. One evening when she had not come home by 9 p.m., I left her meat and bone in her night cage. Sometime later she sneaked in, ate half the meat, took the bone, demolished it, and called in on Babu Lal, who was cooking his supper, before vanishing into the night. By then I knew from experience that if hand-reared animals cannot find the person they are looking for, they are liable to depart with some familiar household article. Prince had taken my camera lens case, Harriet my shoes, the monkeys my spectacles, and you (repeatedly) whatever you could find. I therefore suspected that Tara would have visited my bed, which was next to her night cage. Soon inspection revealed that she had indeed run true to form. Having torn a hole in my mosquito net, she had decamped with my blanket, which she had shredded in a mustard-field fifty yards away. Later that night, at about 11 p.m., I was woken by a *Prusten*, and in the dim light of a torch I saw an ingratiating face peering at me from a distance of about eighteen inches. Tracks revealed that in approaching me she had given your bed a wide berth, for she still accorded you full dominance on the verandah.

Her movements now became impossible to control, as an inner compulsion drew her into the forest every

Cooling off in the river

Harriet, Tara and Eelie return home from a walk

morning. Because I could see that a final break was coming, I asked the Forest Department for permission to fit her with a radio collar, so that I would be able to keep track of her movements; but they in their wisdom refused. So it was that in January 1978, when she was twenty months old, there came the parting of our ways.

The morning of the fifth was cold and clear. Since the early hours she had been calling fitfully, eager to go out and join the male with whom she had been consorting. As always, when I opened the door of her cage, you and Harriet were waiting to set off on our walk.

The tigress went over to the electricity pylon and sprayed on it, but with greater force than usual, perhaps reflecting her pent-up emotions. As you and Harriet completed your ritual urinations, she went and crouched in the ploughed field. You followed her – but then came a drastic break with tradition, for when she charged you in play, for the first time in your life you turned tail and ran to me for protection. Though you looked as sprightly as ever, nature had warned you that your powers were waning, and that it was no longer safe for you to stand up to the tigress, who at over two hundred and fifty pounds was now nearly ten times your weight.

Less than two weeks later, on 16 January, she went out of your life for ever. When I released her that morning, she embraced me from the plinth of the verandah. But soon after we had set out on our morning tour, she branched off on her own along the Escarpment, and finally severed the connection with her childhood companions.

I cannot be sure how long your memory of her lasted. Of course you came with me when I went out looking for her, and I am sure that at first you were able to distinguish her scent from that of the other tigers on the range. Certainly you recognised it four months later, when you and Harriet went up to a tiger's spray on a jamun tree. Some droplets had trickled down onto the grass, and when you sniffed them a frown creased your brow before you did a token urination on the base of the tree, exactly as you had in the past on the electricity pylon. When Harriet also upended her posterior to spray below the tiger's mark, I had no doubt at all that both of you recognised your former comrade.

After that, I imagine, your recollection of her must gradually have faded, for she never returned to the farm or made contact with me. But perhaps you would like to have a brief outline of her subsequent career, for in some ways it has been as remarkable as your own. As I write, she is still alive and well at the age of twelve, and has borne three families – a total of seven cubs – to the wild tiger I call Tara's Male.

For many years, whenever I came across her in the forest, she would move away, ignoring my calls. But of late there has been a change in her behaviour which I find both striking and moving. Now, when I call, she stops, looks towards me, and sometimes even advances a pace or two in my direction – something that no ordinary wild tiger would ever dream of doing. It is as if she is accepting me not just as a dimly-remembered friend from long ago, but as a real companion. And the fact that I belong to a different world, but still am able to get through to her, is due in no small measure to the role which you, dear Eelie, played at the beginning of her life.

NINE

Growing Old

Almost imperceptibly our routines changed. Living with you day after day, week after week, month after month, I scarcely noticed you growing older. But of course time was rolling on; and since seven years of a dog's life are the equivalent of one year for a human, in due course I had to accept the fact that you were already in late middle age.

One major change was thrust upon us by fate within months of Tara's departure. First Mameena, the single cub of Harriet's second pregnancy, was run over and killed by a train, and then Harriet herself was found dead, apparently poisoned, in the long grass scarcely a hundred yards from the farm. For me it was a bitter double blow to have my leopard project brought to so premature an end. You, I think, felt the tragedy less, for although you and Harriet had always remained on friendly terms, she had been largely preoccupied with her own affairs in recent months, and you had seen less of her.

Nothing, however, could stop the process of growing old. You, who had always fearlessly led the way into the jungle, past tiger kills and sprays, now refused to venture into the forest beyond the Junction Bridge. You still took pleasure in walks along more open pathways, but instinct told you that, with your own physical powers declining, it was not safe for you to move through thick undergrowth, or tall grass, where the scent of tigers almost always lingered. The result was that I took to putting you on a lead as we set out – with the double object of encouraging you to come and keeping you close to me – and then letting you loose, to run ahead, as we turned for home.

Your wisdom was strikingly illustrated by an event that took place in April 1979, when you were about eight and a half years old, or sixty in human terms. One morning you were so reluctant to come walking that, soon after we had set out, you slipped your collar and ran home alone. Jackson and I went on, but as we came back through some tall grass I caught a glimpse of a tigress known to me as the Median. Already we were suspicious of this animal, for she had shown exceptional aggression against humans – and in fact a year later she became a full-blooded man-eater, killing five people, among them my assistant tracker, on whom she jumped only a couple of hundred yards from the house. Even at this early meeting I sensed something unusual in her behaviour, for although she left the path as Jackson and I went quietly past, I saw her crouching low in the grass less than ten feet away. Most tigers would have moved off, but there she stayed, scowling at me, and immediately I realised that you had had a miraculous escape: had you been with us, trotting on ahead as usual on the return journey, she would almost certainly have grabbed you. Was it pure luck that had saved you, or some intuition far beyond the reach of my own limited perception?

Sometimes I regretted that I had not kept one of your puppies to carry on your line; but when I reflected on the idea, I realised that my close contact with wild animals, and my over-riding desire that they should live naturally, had made me more and more reluctant to keep pets. (You, of course, were the great exception, but you were unique.) Another thing which influenced me was the fact that when you became pregnant, you were at an obvious disadvantage in your daily rough-housing with the young leopards. By the time Tara arrived I realised that if you were to retain your full ability to deal with big cats, your power of domination must not be undermined by the distractions of having to protect your own offspring. I therefore put you on the pill, with the result that you had no more litters.

As one young naturalist put it, your long association with the leopards and the tiger turned you more or less into an honorary cat, and one mark of your new status was your habit of creeping up on people to whom you had taken a dislike in a particularly cat-like manner. One day, for instance, you stalked the Forest Range Officer from the Park Headquarters at Dudhwa and bit him in the leg, which embarrassed me greatly at the time.

I am glad to be able to recall that a new interest enlivened your declining years. During the summer of 1979 a small cat was found abandoned after a grass fire at Bellraien, some twenty miles from Tiger Haven. With typical ignorance the forest authorities claimed it was a leopard cub, but fortunately I happened to be in the area and saw at once that it was a fishing cat, or rather kitten, hardly a week old. The forest staff said that it would not feed, and one of them tried to solve the problem by pouring a jug of milk over its upturned face. The kitten spluttered and nearly choked. I begged them to give it to me, and after some hesitation, they agreed.

An adult fishing cat – *Felis viverrina* – is about double the size of a domestic cat and has very elegant markings – rows of elongated dark spots on a grey-brown background. This kitten, however, was little more than a ball of spotted fluff. Back at home, I was rather apprehensive about how you might react to it, as you had not had a family for three years, and might have lost your maternal instincts. Far from it: the moment I put it down in front of you, you accepted it, and allowed it to climb all over you, licking it clean just as its mother would have done.

I named the kitten Tiffany, and she grew well on buffalo milk fed to her from a dropper. Then, after a month, she vanished. No amount of searching revealed her whereabouts until you, clearly wondering what all the fuss was about, appointed yourself as guide and led me to her. There she was, standing in the shallow stream under the Junction Bridge, and dabbling for fish with her tiny paws. Once again I was amazed by the genetic inheritance of animals: here, in this tiny creature, which had been deprived of its mother almost at birth, I could see at work the same instinct that leads young tigers and leopards to hunt. No other creature – merely her genes – had told her she was a fishing cat, and that fishing was her trade.

Throughout her association with us, she retained a preference for fish, but she would also eat meat. As she grew up she began to stalk the peafowl and junglefowl for which I scattered grain in the mornings, and it must have been thoroughly frustrating for her when the larger birds ignored her deadly, undercover approaches. She used to come for walks with us, but her forelegs were so short and stubby that she tired easily. With her short tail – poor for balancing – she was a singularly inept climber of trees. Her one great skill was fishing, and when we came to a stream she would sit on the bank and scoop fish out with the greatest ease – even though ignorant foresters were willing to believe that she and her kind dangled their tails in the water as lures.

Tiffany was completely unrestrained, apart from sleeping in a room at night, and at the age of about a year she found herself a mate in the shape of a large male who frequented local tiger kills. After that she took to the wild, appearing only for an occasional meal in the morning, and sometimes, depending on the pressure of her other social activities, not returning at all for fifteen days on end. When she did come, she would appear at first light and peer into my room, calling piteously, and then, as I emerged, rub herself against my legs until I felt I was the only person in the world who mattered – although at the end of her meal she would disappear without a backward glance. As soon as I fed her, you too would turn up, and get a few pieces from her bowl, although the purpose of your presence was more social than gastronomic, for (as I have said) you never much liked raw meat, especially as you grew older.

Early one winter morning a loud bawling started up from inside a water tank in which I had once kept a young crocodile. Tiffany's young kitten had fallen in, and there seemed no way of getting it out, for no sooner did we rush to one end of the tank than she swam to the other, while her mother ran agitatedly up and down the parapet, and you copied her movements on the ground. At last we hit on the idea of laying a plank sloping down into the water, and went away. When we came back, the kitten had climbed out, but after getting that fright it would not come near the house again.

During the monsoon I would sometimes see mother and child hunting in the shallow flood waters which surrounded us, and at night they would communicate with a chattering call rather like that of an Indian fox; but unlike Elsa, the sociable lioness who brought her cubs to Joy Adamson, these solitary cats, although willing to maintain a personal relationship with a human being, tended to keep their offspring away.

Over the next few months we continued to hear their calls at night. Some of these were undoubtedly contact calls with a male, for a year later Tiffany appeared with twins. Hard as I tried to get to know these youngsters, they never became really trusting, and a tenuous association soon languished. But Tiffany herself continued to visit us, and proved herself a true cat of two worlds: one morning she fed with you behind the buildings at Tiger Haven, as usual, and a few nights later I photographed her scavenging a tiger kill in the forest.

In the winter of 1983 she appeared looking very bloated. I realised that she must be about to produce a larger-than-normal family, for cats show very little outward sign of pregnancy until the final stages. I expected her to give birth in the long grass beyond the Junction Bridge, where she had had her other families; and in the middle of March, when she did not come to the farm for three days, I reckoned the new family must have arrived.

Then, on 18 March, tragedy struck. At midnight I heard a single loud squawk from the direction of the long grass, and two days later, when you ran off to investigate why vultures were descending on that area, we found the demolished carcase of a large fishing cat. The head was bigger than Tiffany's, with different markings, and a cavity in one of the molars suggested that the animal had been fairly old. I concluded that it must have been the father, trying to defend his offspring against a tiger, but the rest of the body had been eaten by vultures, and it was impossible to tell exactly what had happened.

Having found the tracks of Tara and her single cub outside the grass of the maternity ward, I concluded that the tigress had killed the fishing cat to protect her own daughter.

That night a single, chattering bark sounded from near the bridge, but Tiffany never returned, and the best I could hope was that, demoralised by the tigress's attack, she had carried her cubs away, one by one, to safer surroundings. So ended another unique association, and one in which you had taken an integral part.

Just like humans who grow old, you became steadily slower and more conservative, and in your last couple of years you would not stray from the immediate precincts of Tiger Haven. One of your great pleasures was to climb laboriously the steep steps to the upper verandah, and from that comfortable eminence watch the peafowl and junglefowl feeding on grain, and the chital eating cut fig leaves on the flat, open ground in front of the house: a peaceful pageant in which individuals might change, but life went on. And if your legs had become infirm, there was nothing wrong with your nose: whenever wind-borne scent told you that there was a tiger somewhere close in the forest, you would set up a loud, sustained barking from the safety of your home territory on the near side of the Junction Bridge.

If I am to be honest, I must admit that in later years you became rather spoilt. By then your friend Kharak Bahadur had left us, but you had struck up a close relationship with his successor Auro Bindo, who would spend hours coaxing you to eat. This was just as well, for you had become extremely fussy about food, and often when I gave you your dinner you would just look at the dish and move off, as though the sight of it disgusted you. I knew perfectly well that you were doing it to annoy me, and that as soon as I was out of the way you would probably start to eat; even so, I was glad when Auro Bindo managed to tempt your appetite by feeding you small pieces of meat with his hands.

Your feud with Abou Bakr the goat continued to the end. His final act of sacrilege so far as you were concerned came one day when we were sitting down to an afternoon cup of tea. Goose-stepping up to the verandah to get his usual chapati, he stamped on your right ear, crumpling its cartilage and leaving it with a permanent droop. A few days later you got your own back by creeping under the table at tea-time and giving him a sharp bite in the leg.

Your attitude towards tourists remained inscrutably non-committal. During cold winter evenings your mattress had a place of honour in front of the log fire that we keep blazing in the drawing-room, and you would tolerate guests unless they stepped on your bedding or tried to patronise you. If that happened, you would come to me and lead the way out of the warm room to your little bed on the upstairs verandah, next to mine.

Visitors were always amazed by the discrimination with which you would watch screenings of the Anglia Television film 'The Leopard that Changed its Spots', in which you played a strong supporting role. The moment Harriet appeared, you would get up and go behind the screen in search of your former companion, but when the film moved to Sri Lanka and showed the wild leopards there, you would start barking at the sight of your natural enemies. Here was final proof – as if I needed any – that all your life you had recognised my big cats as individual beings, rather than as members of a species.

Your end, when it came, arrived with inexorable finality. You were in your fourteenth year when a cancer appeared on your breast and took over with unbelievable violence. Your black-rimmed eyes were still as bright as buttons, but they became tinged with unutterable pain until, in April 1984, a merciful death closed them for ever.

With your passing, a part of my own life had come to a close. My inseparable companion for over thirteen years, you had been an integral part of my experiments with the great cats, and you had contributed immeasurably to my understanding of their nature. Your strong yet sympathetic personality formed a unique bridge between the artificial, domestic world of man and the immutable but much-tortured world of nature. For me, you were the ultimate dog. And although Tara was certainly still alive, and Prince may have been, with your death an era had ended.

We laid you to rest beside the spot where the remains of Juliette and Harriet were already interred, and where I myself plan to be buried one day. Thirteen years ago, you had arrived unwanted and unloved; and now, as you departed, I wept beside your grave.

So there it is. I said I would write about our time together so that I could share it with others, and although the task has often made me sad, I have enjoyed it too. Now I must say farewell. But you may rest assured that I will never forget you, wherever your spirit may be.

Your lifelong friend

Billy